Blacker the Berry

By

Eddie J Martin

Janice Willow

Born: Detroit, Mich.
Age: 28
Race: Blk
Ht.: 5'11"
Wt.: 143
Breast: 39, waist: 23, hips: 35

Schools: Downing Elementary, Rosa Park High School

Sports: Soccer, basketball, volleyball, karate, judo, mountain climbing

Employment: Smell So Sweet Have-A-Dashers, 1993–1994
United States Air Force, 1994–2005
Federal Government, 2005–Present

Expertise: Assassin

Blacker the Berry

Chapter 1

HE WATCHED HER as she walked naked across the room to the bathroom.

"Did anyone ever tell you that you are one fine black woman? Did anyone ever tell you that, Janice?"

"Yes, I've been told that, mostly by men before we made love, not after."

"Before or after, you are one fine woman."

"Are you trying to get me back into bed, Bart? If so, it's working. Give me a minute!"

At that moment her phone rang, and she walked over to the dresser, looked at the caller ID, saw it was from the agency, and decided to let it go to voice mail.

Bart's rang right after hers, and she looked at him and he at her. Looked at his caller ID and said to Janice, "It's the agency."

"Don't answer it. We'll get back to them, maybe this afternoon."

"It could be an emergency."

"It's always an emergency. Don't answer it," Janice said.

"Sir, I can't seem to reach Willow or Agent Bart, but I did leave a message." Agent Stone was addressing Agent Jenkins, head of the FBI special branch.

Janice Willow had been working for the agency for over three years after the two agents recruited her against her will. Agents Stone and Jenkins had learned that Willow was a killer and had killed over a dozen people that they knew of. They decided to use her for their own purpose instead of putting her in jail. As Agent Jenkins put it, "Willow belongs to us now."

After being on over four cases and showing her worth…there was just one small problem. She loved to kill. She not only killed the ones she was told to kill; she killed others she wasn't supposed to. Willow, they found, had been a killing machine since long before there was a Jaws. Give her that Beretta and that Japanese throwing knife and she would tackle anybody. Throw in the karate and judo and you've got one hell of a woman. They could only go back as far as her entering the military, but they believed that the killing started well before that.

At 10:00 a.m. Willow walked into Agent Jenkins's office, thirty minutes after Agent Bart. Agent Stone was also there.

"Sorry I'm late, sir, but I got held up on the way here, and I had to give my report to the police."

"If it was anyone else, Janice, I would have said a likely story," Jenkins said. "But since it's you, should I ask what happened?"

"To make a long story short, on the way here, there was an attempted carjacking on me, and it didn't go the way the carjackers hoped it would."

"Let me ask you this, Janice. Were there any deaths involved?"

"No, sir, but the ambulance was called. You should be getting a call soon."

"OK, OK. Now let's get down to our business. Before you arrived we were explaining to Agent Bart what the assignment was. In short you won't be the lead this time but the backup to Agent Bart."

"No disrespect to Agent Bart, but, sir, I never go on any assignment with anyone, and you know I work alone. And to back up—"

"I know, Janice, and if there were anyone else, I'd send them, but as of right now, you are it."

"You won't tell me about this assignment I'm supposed to be backup on?"

"Bart can explain it to you on the flight. That'll be leaving in just about one hour and thirty minutes from now."

"No time to go back home and pack?" Janice asked.

"Grab what you need at your next stop. Plus we'll have most of what you need when you get there. Any questions?"

"Who's in charge of this operation?" Bart asked.

"I see you never worked with Agent Willow before, and I'll just say this. No one's in charge, and once you're out in the field, you'll see why. Let's just say you'll be working together and leave it at that."

Chapter 2

ON THE PLANE Bart and Willow were sitting side by side, each with a drink in their hands. Willow reclined her seat and said, "I'm listening."

Bart started, "We're on our way to Europe with a fuel stop in Florida. I'll be changing planes in Ireland, and you'll continue on to Germany. The next time you'll see me, I'll be undercover. I'll contact you."

"You want to tell me what you'll be undercover as, Bart?"

"A terrorist. What else, Janice? I thought you knew. I'll go for my training in the hills of Afghanistan and make my way to Germany and recruit you somewhere along the way. So you just sit tight until I get there."

"I'm not too good at sitting tight, but I'll try. How long we talking about?"

"Three to six weeks. They know I have military experience in my background, so they may even cut the training time because of it."

Willow walked into her twelfth-floor suite at the Barter Hoff Hotel in Frankfurt, two bedrooms, bar, and large-screen TV. Two lounge chairs and couch, baths, plus kitchenette. Her patio was overlooking the park and downtown Frankfurt. Right under the patio was the hotel swimming pool with patio chairs and café. And in one of the bedrooms, there was an assortment of clothes, from the casual to the dinner dress. Undergarments and shoes, all in her size. All in her favorite colors and in one of the shoeboxes were Willow's Beretta and Japanese throwing knife. The agency didn't forget a thing.

Chapter 3

AFTER TRAVELING TO Turkey, Bart was contacted by members of the Taliban and made it overland by Jeep and then by mule and camel. On the fifth day, they arrived at the training camp somewhere in the mountains of Afghanistan. There he saw approximately three hundred to four hundred men in various stages of training. Out of the twenty men Bart made the trip with, he was the only one singled out to speak to the commander. Bart a.k.a. Raymond Massey was brought in front of the commander and asked why he was there and why he wanted to join this group.

"I feel the Afghan people are getting a raw deal, and I felt I could be of some service. Besides you're the only war that's going on, and you know I am a warrior. Plus, the pay is good!"

"That's right. You did spend time in the military, but you were kicked out. Would you like to tell me about that?"

"You already know one of the Moslem brothers was getting harassed, and I stepped in. A person got killed, and I was blamed for his death. I was convicted, served three years in prison, and received a dishonorable discharge from the military."

"I understand you were a trainer and DI."

"Yes, sir, I did all that for a country that didn't seem to understand, so here I am."

"From here on out, your name will no longer be Raymond Massey but Co Mo Dee, your Moslem name. Even if you are only in it for the money, you still will have to have the Moslem name for the ones that are in it for the faith, you understand. It'll be our secret. Since you were a trainer and explosive expert, we'll start you off there, as a trainer for us."

Four weeks later, Co Mo Dee was again called into the commander's tent. "Mo Dee, we find your talents here are being wasted. Not that we don't love your work, but we feel you could do us more justice someplace else."

"And where would that be, sir?"

"In the city, maybe Germany, Frankfurt."

"Why there, may I ask?"

"We have people in Frankfurt, and we could use a man of your talents to shore up the setup we already have there."

"Wherever you think I'll be of the most service," Mo Dee said. "When do I leave?"

"Two days. It'll give you time to get briefed and so on. There is also a sum of money we want you to deliver to the leader there."

Meanwhile, Willow was in Frankfurt, having a ball. Shopping, sightseeing, swimming in the hotel pool. Breakfasts in her room, sometimes lunch. And dinner in the hotel restaurant. Men were always coming over to her table, introducing themselves. Sometimes even women came. Some she went with, and some she didn't. She made sure each was leaving within a few days of the encounter, and it worked out very well.

After about the fifth week, she started worrying about Bart. She called Agent Stone, and he told her to sit tight and that he'd show up. That really wasn't her style. She could do only so much shopping and screwing, especially if she wasn't screwing Bart.

But then again the airline pilot she met the other week, she was OK. Willow was really getting bored. Not doing her job for long periods of time did that.

Then it happened, at about three o'clock in the morning. She woke up in a cold sweat. Her hair felt like it was moving on its own. Her fingers and nails were getting longer. Her ears, nose, and mouth seemed like they were stretching out of shape. Teeth were getting longer and were below her bottom lip. Hair was forming all over her body, and her breasts had dwindled down to nothing. Skin had turned from ivory to black. Feet were wider, longer, and harrier than usual.

"It's come back, my demon, the Medusa."

Whenever "it" came back, she knew she had to kill somebody, anybody.

Three floors below a couple returned to their room after celebrating the night away. Going into the room, he tried carrying her across the threshold. Both were laughing and stumbling on the way, and they left the door partly cracked. Willow came in right behind them, closed the door, and watched them go into the bedroom. They dropped on the bed, and both looked like they were out until the lady got up and went into the bathroom and threw up in the toilet.

Willow walked over to the bed where the man was laid out, leaned over him with her knife, and cut his throat. She then walked into the bath where the lady was on her knees, head in the toilet and barfing and saying, "Oh Lord, oh Lord, never again. Never again."

Willow stood over her, grabbed her hair, and pulled her head back so her throat was exposed. The lady noticed her just before Willow cut her throat, and all that came from her mouth was a scream that never materialized. Willow let her head drop back down in the toilet and left the apartment and went back to her room, got in bed, and slept like a baby the rest of the night.

At 9:00 a.m. that same morning, Willow woke, got on the house phone, and ordered breakfast. Coffee, orange juice, toast, and grapefruit. She took a shower, and thirty minutes later, there was a knock at the door. Willow answered it in her negligée; it was the steward with her breakfast.

While setting up the tray, she started telling Willow about the killing. She was a talker and told Willow everything. A couple of the girls had quit when they heard of it; they had just clocked in.

"Who found the bodies?"

"A maid. She went by their door and saw it was partly open and went in to investigate, and there they were, one on the bed and the other in the bathroom with her head in the toilet. Call when you want someone to pick up your tray, miss." And she left.

Willow poured herself a cup of coffee and helped herself to a half a piece of toast and walked out on the patio. Police cars, a hearse, and CSI vans were all there. She expected they'd be calling on her in a little while. Well, maybe not. After all there were over two thousand rooms in this hotel, and that had happened three floors below.

Willow walked back into the bath and looked at herself in the mirror. Ebony skin, long, black curly hair, long neck, wide lips. Straight nose and picture-perfect, large black eyes. Breasts that were standing out at attention, no sagging yet. She opened up her negligée and looked at her body.

No spring chicken here, she thought, *a full-figured woman.* Not bad for a broad of twenty-eight, but nothing like earlier.

If she had to guess, how many people had she killed since the beginning?

Twenty, thirty, I've lost count. Maybe if my parents would have gotten me help when I asked…Well, that's water under the bridge now. For the help I didn't get, I ended up killing my father and would have killed my mother if she hadn't died first. The Medusa, that's what I call my demon, and I never know when it'll come out. Mostly in the dead of night or early in the morning. Maybe I would have been better off if the Feds had put me away. At least for the dead, it would have been, but it seems like I am of use to someone.

"The things I do for my country."

A week later Willow received a call from Bart. "You moved?"

"Yes, there were complications at the hotel. You in town?"

"Yes, I've been here for a few days now. Things I had to take care of. I'll tell you about it when we meet. Where are you located?"

Bart knocked on the door an hour later, at 8 Stryker, a small, quiet cottage on a dead-end street in the middle of Frankfurt. Willow looked out of the peephole, saw Bart, and opened the door. Once the door was closed, they grabbed each other and embraced, kissed, and headed straight for the bedroom.

Willow lay in Bart's arms, both spent and sweating. "I've missed you," Willow said.

"And I missed you," Bart said.

"I especially miss this." And Willow grabbed Bart's penis.

"You sure don't mind showing your affection."

"That's right, Bart. That's what life is all about."

"By the way, my name is no longer Bart. I've been given the name of Co Mo Dee. They felt it would be more acceptable to the other brothers."

"And how did you pull that off?"

"Believe it or not, all of them are not in the fighting because they believe in what they do. It's about the good old American dollar bill. They see I'm one of those."

"What is your job here, and where do I come in?"

"They had me deliver money to the safe house. From what I've learned, there's ten in the cell, and there's at least three areas they plan on hitting here in Frankfurt."

"Did you deliver the money?"

"I did. As you would guess, they are monitoring me, and I feel it could have been a setup. There is one thing that I'm not too proud of."

"What's that, Bart?"

"I had to kill someone that I was told was a spy. I don't know if he was or not, but I shot him in the back of the head. Whatever tests they put me through, I guess I passed, that time."

"What's next?"

"I get the feeling they're looking at the train system; we'll have to ask Agent Stone how far he wants to go with this. You'll have to do that. I'm watched to close. This particular cell has run havoc in five countries so far and has been very successful up to this point. Every time we get close to them, they vanish. Why they put me with these guys is probably because of my nationality. Eventually I feel they'll be sending me to the States."

"Uh-huh," Janice said and turned over and kissed Bart on his chest and then his naval and then his penis.

Bart felt such a shock that his toes went rigid; he grabbed the headboard and put so much pressure on it it nearly broke. "Good God," he murmured.

Chapter 4

"DON'T YOU THINK you're taking a chance, Commander? Why not kill him right here?"

"Japel, sometimes it's best to know what the other side is thinking and who his contacts are. It was a bit of luck that one of our men recognize the infidel we call Co Mo Dee. I think he would have gotten away with his charade otherwise."

"How far are you going to let him infiltrate our cell?"

"Just far enough to let him hang himself. The cell has been informed, and they're watching him."

"What about the girl he recently made contact with?"

"She may be his only contact; it didn't take him long to get to her."

"Why do you think he killed the spy?"

"He had no choice. If he hadn't, I was prepared to kill him right on the spot. It's like this, Japel. We know that they're getting close to the cell, but we need to find out how close. We'll find out what we can from Co Mo Dee by following him, and if that won't do, then torture him and find out that way."

"What about the girl?"

"The same goes for her. Capture, torture, and then kill her. One, two, three. After that we'll move the cell to Paris or one of the other countries we have targeted."

Agent Stone entered Agent Jenkins's office and informed him about the Frankfurt operation. "Bart just made contact with Janice. He's in place with the cell there. He thinks they're going to hit the Bon-Hoff first, and they want him to deliver the explosives. Do we give him the word to go through with it?"

"Let me think about that one, Stone. If he goes through with it, we're talking about a lot of people dying versus ten people in the cell. The Bon-Hoff may hold a few hundred. I don't think it'll be worth it. Plus our allies won't think so, either. I think we should bust them now, and if Bart's in the bunch, we'll just have to bust him also and work it out afterward."

"There is no way they won't believe it was Bart that finked them out."

"Maybe so but we just can't take the chance," Jenkins said.

A week later Germany's elite force broke into the cell where they were held up. Six cell members were taken into custody or killed; Bart was suspected right away, and the remaining group apprehended him. In a ship on the river, Bart was hanging by chains from the ceiling with only his toes touching the floor. There was a six-foot bamboo cane he was being whipped with.

"Who do you work for?" the cell leader asked him. "What did you tell them?"

Bart denied everything.

"It won't get any better," the cell leader said.

Next came the water treatment. Over half his men were incarcerated, and he wasn't too happy about it. Sometimes he watered Bart more than he intended to, and it got into Bart's face, and Bart spit in his face. The leader got so mad until the knife he had in his belt he grabbed, and before he knew it, stuck it in Bart's midsection and pulled it up to his neck and back down again.

Bart's eyes went wide, and he murmured, "Damn."

The leader realized what he had done and knew there was nothing he could learn now. "Go get the girl," he said to his men, "and bring her here. She'll tell us what we want to know."

Two hours later the men were back with Willow. The first thing she saw was Bart hanging from the ceiling, naked. The front of his chest cut open down to his penis. That beautiful penis she loved so.

She screamed and started crying, saying, "What did you do to him?"

In reality, Willow felt little because she lacked real feelings for anyone. It was true she liked Bart, but she had had a lot of Barts that she'd loved and murdered. She would miss him, but that was the way it went. Now to send the four right behind him.

When they had picked her up, they had made a couple of mistakes. First, they hadn't bound her hands or otherwise contained her. Second, they hadn't realized how dangerous she was.

The leader came up to her and slapped her face and told her that she would tell them everything. He tossed her over in the corner so she would have a good view of Bart. The leader and one of his men left the room. That left two with Willow. Before the leader left, he had told his men to bind her and put her beside her man. One of the men found some twine and came toward her; the other one picked up a chair lying on the floor. The one with the twine grabbed Willow by the arm to pull her up, but as she came off the floor, in the other hand, she had her knife and swiped it across his throat. He grabbed his throat and just stood there, spouting blood.

Willow did not bother about him but turned her attention toward the other one. He had turned toward them, and before he could make another move, she had tossed the knife into his throat. He fell with his hand on the knife handle, trying to pull it out. Willow helped him by pushing it in farther and giving it a turn. After retrieving her knife and the revolvers the men had, she looked up at Bart and shook her head.

"You were all right, Bart. I'll miss you."

Willow went outside the room and waited. Not long the leader and his man came back. The leader went in the room first and his man right behind him. Willow walked out of her hiding place and shot him in the back and the leader in his leg. The leader went down, holding his leg; she walked over to the other one and shot him once in the head.

The leader looked up at her in disbelief and said, "How did you?"

"Never mind about that. You've got some talking to do. Take your time, please."

It took a while, but they had all the tools there to make it happen. First she strung him up where Bart was hanging, cut his clothes off, and started to work on him with her Japanese throwing knife. At first he didn't answer her questions, and she was happy about that. After the third hour, he was telling her everything she wanted to know. That is after the forth finger and third toe were cut off. Cuts on his body and his left eye nearly cut out but not quite. Both ears cut off and one punctured eardrum.

It wasn't until she started cutting one of his balls off that he really started singing. After he said what she wanted to hear and believed to be true, she cut it off anyway, along with his penis, and after she had gotten everything she thought she was going to get from him, she really got busy.

His last words were, "You black bitch."

Two days later, back in DC…

"I received word from Janice Willow," Agent Stone relayed to Agent Jenkins. "She said that Bart was dead, and she confirmed his death. The cell was eliminated, but the people that sent him to his death were still out there. What are her instructions?"

"Too bad about Bart," Jenkins said. "He was a good agent. We'll bring his body back if possible, and then I think we'll go after the ones that made it happen. The commander."

Chapter 5

JAPEL ENTERED THE commander's tent and relayed to him what he knew about the cell in Frankfurt.

"The cell is no more, sir. All are either in jail or dead, including the leader and Co Mo Dee."

"What about the girl, Japel? Is there no mention of her?"

"No, sir, the last I heard of her was when the leader was having her picked up to question her. And that was the last time I spoke to him."

"Japel, tell the men to abandon camp. I have a feeling we're going to be attacked."

"What gives you that idea, sir? We've been here for over a year without incident."

"Yes, that was when our main cell was intact, but things have happened since then. Plus, we don't know what the leader has told them."

"The leader would never talk," Japel said.

"We all will talk under the right interrogation, even the leader. Now start breaking camp. I want to be out of here by tomorrow morning."

That next afternoon as the commander and his men reached the mountains, they looked back toward their old camp, and there was an inferno. Bombs rained down on the camp for what seemed like hours; they could see no aircraft, but they knew they were there. The camp was demolished.

Japel looked at the commander, his mouth open, and started to say something, then thought better of it. The commander glanced at the camp and then continued up the mountain.

The caves they were looking for took the rest of the day to get to. Some provisions were already there, being that they had used the area before. The cave was actually two connected together: a sleeping and cooking area and a private area for the commander. Nothing like the old camp with tents for everyone, but then they were alive, and that meant a lot. For sure if they would have stayed there, they all would have been wiped out.

He knew Japel was wondering how he knew they were going to be attacked…Well, that was why he was the commander. His job was to predict things like that. The leader of the Frankfurt cell should have predicted what would happen to his cell, predicted Co Mo Dee, but he hadn't, and it was all on him. Now he had to replace the Frankfurt cell with another; it would not be easy because of their kill rate. But they had people standing in line to be martyred, to get to heaven and their virgins and pots of gold. They had used that same cave when they had gone to war with the Russians and now with the Americans.

Looks like our fate is to war. I don't think it'll ever end, but my job is to fight day by day and protect and train my men. I must have Japel find out information about Co Mo Dee's assistant. If she's not dead, too.

She was the key to the demise of the Frankfurt cell. The commander knew he shouldn't make it so personal, but he was partly responsible for not killing Co Mo Dee when he had the chance. No one would bring it up to him, but no one had to. He knew.

Meanwhile back in DC, agents Stone and Jenkins were discussing the hit on the Afghanistan camp. Stone said before they bombed the camp, they sent a drone over to see if there was any activity. It had spotted none, so the generals had decided to bomb the camp anyway, just to let them know they were on their case and one day would catch them home.

"We believe they abandoned their camp and departed some time during the night or early that morning. Where is Janice now? Still in Germany?" Jenkins asked.

"Yes, sir, awaiting instructions. Have you decided on her going after the commander yet? He's probably holed up in those caves by now, and it'll be hard to get to him. What we need is a way to lure him out of those mountains. Any ideas?"

Chapter 6

WILLOW HAD MADE her way into the hills of Afghanistan. She had decided not to wait on instructions from agents Stone and Jenkins. She was dressed as a typical Afghan woman, burka and all. She even painted her face a darker color, darker than it was. She was traveling with ten other women who were headed to the mountains to be with their men. Willow said she was also meeting her man. There were at least ten children, the eldest being no more than eight.

The mountains looked no more than a half day's walk, but she soon found out that looks were deceiving. The mountains looked closer than they really were. Once they reached the first mountain, they were told that there were two more to cross.

On the fifth night, five robbers attacked, but money was not all they wanted. They started taking the women aside and raping them. When it was Willow's turn, one grabbed her by the hand and pulled her behind some boulders. He threw her down on the ground and started pulling off her burka and pulling down his trousers. Once he was on top of her, skin to skin, that's when he felt it, cold steel. Willow had her Japanese throwing knife out and to his midsection, where she pushed and turned. He was about to let out a scream, but she managed to put her scarf in his mouth. She pushed him off her right at the moment another robber came around the boulder. The knife she still held, with no hesitation, was thrown into his throat. He dropped his weapon and dropped to his knees, holding his throat.

Willow immediately picked up his AR-15 and headed for the camp. The robber that was holding the other women at bay was the first one she shot. Another came running around another boulder where he had been in the process of raping, and Willow unloaded six rounds into him.

The fifth robber heard the commotion and got off the woman he had, holding a knife on her. He started to run back to the camp, but he had no weapon other then his knife. He had left his AK back at the camp with the guard, thinking he wouldn't need it. He grabbed the woman by her hair and put her in front of him with the knife to her throat and walked with her in front of him.

The women, in the meantime, had picked up the dead robbers' weapons and were looking around, wondering what to do next.

Willow knew there were five robbers, and four were down, so she said to the others, "There is one more. Where is he?"

At that moment, he and his hostage walked out, and he noticed his comrades dead on the ground and assumed the others were, too.

"You will let me leave, or I will kill this woman," he said.

The women all looked at one another and started to encircle him. Some had the dead robbers' ARs, and others had their knives.

"Let me go," he said again. "I swear by the name of Allah I will kill her."

The ring around the robber was getting smaller; the blade he held at her neck drew blood. The women kept coming. The robber saw that there was no way they were going to stop, so he dropped his knife and dropped to his knees, releasing his hostage, and covered his head and started pleading for them not to kill him. The ones with the rifles started beating him, and the ones with knives started stabbing him. The ones with nothing hit and kicked him with whatever they had.

Once they were finished, Willow walked over to him and put three rounds of the AR-15 into him.

By the time the women had gotten to the third mountain range, they had elected Willow their official leader, and in so doing they talked to her freely and openly. One's husband was a leader and wanted to be a martyr. Two wives in this life weren't enough for him. But on the other hand, if he died, she, being his widow, would be looked up to and given all his possessions. She believed she would rather have the possessions.

Another knew her husband was dead but just wanted the professions. A few of the others were sincere as far as she could tell and just wanted to be with their husbands. Those who had kids, wherever the women went the kids followed.

There was one bit of information she thought she could use. One of the men's wives had gotten killed, but he had no knowledge of it. The marriage had been arranged, and he had never seen her before. Willow thought that she could just as well be that wife; better still she found out that he was close to this leader she was seeking. His name was Japel. From what she learned, he was third in line to the leader.

Each mountain they came across their members dwindle, women finding their husbands being dead or alive. And Willow's popularity exploded. The women whose husbands were alive stayed with them plus their kids, and the ones whose husbands were dead decided to go alone with Willow.

By the time they reached the area where the commander and his men were holed up, five women had chosen to follow Willow. After the incident with the robbers, the women felt invincible, had found a new worth. There was nothing they couldn't do. A couple got into altercations with men at the previous camps where the men wanted sex after they found out their husbands were dead, which is a no-no unless the women wanted to be touched. With a little help from Willow, the men thought better of it. The one that thought he knew differently ended up with his left eye cut out.

There was one incident one night where three armed men broke into their camp, thinking that they were all women and an easy touch but not knowing they all had weapons. All three men were dead two minutes after they entered the camp. They were relieved of their weapons, and their bodies were tossed over the cliff. Willow's reputation grew!

Chapter 7

JAPEL AND THREE of his men made it back to their old camp to see what they could salvage. The commander felt it was OK and safe, since the place had already been hit once. A couple of tents still stood, and they began going through them. Three miles up, a drone was passing the area, spotted them, and fired as they entered one of the tents. Japel and his men were killed instantly.

Later when the commander got the news, he was not happy and mentioned something about how the infidels would pay. He immediately put a replacement in for Japel. There was to be a meeting with the section leaders in the area that would change the way they were to carry out business from then on and even allow women to be a part of the fighting.

Now that will be something new, the commander thought. *Are we losing the war or just getting desperate, or both?*

But then again he had been hearing of some women headed his way that were handling themselves very well. Killing robbers and taking their weapons—those trying to rape women who belonged to others were dealt with. Japel had mentioned that the woman promised to him was coming this way, but he never said when or much about her.

I wonder, could she by chance be one of the women headed to the camp? We'll see, he thought. *Regardless, she'll have some bad news when she gets here.*

Meanwhile in Washington, DC, agents Jenkins and Stone were discussing the whereabouts of Willow.

"No word from Willow yet?" Agent Jenkins asked Stone.

"No, sir, I think she went after the commander on her own without backup or calling us to let us know what she's doing."

"She did that because she knew what we'd say if she suggested something like that. She'll contact us when she's accomplished her job," Jenkins said. "That is, if she's still alive."

"If I were a betting man, I'd put my money on her," Stone said.

"I'll tell you what, you can have our people be on alert for any signs of her and to give her any assistance she needs."

"If she's in those mountains, I don't know how in the hell she's going to make it," Stone said. "It's a waiting game now."

Agent Jenkins's secretary walked in with a top-secret message that had just been decoded.

"Stone, listen to this. There's going to be a meeting of the top Taliban leaders soon. We're assured of the location. This will be our opportunity to catch all of them together and put a hell of a dent in their operation, slow them down anyway. This is when we could really use Willow."

In the mountains of Afghanistan, the commander was told of the women coming well before they got there; they were spotted a mountain away. Six of them, all carrying weapons of one sort or another. One was much taller than the rest, and he was told she was the leader. Japel's replacement told the commander that they should be there by nightfall.

"Bring them right to me when they arrive," the commander said.

A little after nightfall, Willow and the other women arrived, and they were taken straight to the commander. All six of them stood in front of him, and just as he'd been told, they all looked like his men, although they were women but hardened fighters. He could see why the head commander wanted to have them join the men; if they fought as well as they looked, they were going to be hell to deal with.

"Which one of you is Mafer, the leader?"

No one said anything, and then Willow a.k.a. Mafer stepped forward and said, "I am she."

"You are the one who was promised to Japel? You are his woman?"

"Yes, that's true. Is he here?"

"Japel was killed two days ago. He died for the cause, and he will be missed."

Willow put her head down as if disappointed. "Then my trip was for naught. If you don't mind, my girls and I will stay here a few days and rest up and then head back."

"Stay as long as you like. I'm sure my men will love to have you around."

"Let's understand each other, Commander. The girls are not here for your men's enjoyment. Only if they choose to be handled that way. All are martyrs' wives and should be treated as such, and from what you say about Japel, so am I."

"That's not quite true," he said. "You were promised to Japel, but you never married."

"Until I am promised to another, I'll always feel as though I'm Japel's woman."

"We'll discuss this another time, Mafer. Until then we'll find you a place to bed down and feed you and talk in the morning."

After they left, the commander sat down by his fire, took out his pipe, and thought about the women he just met, especially Mafer. He would not mind having her for himself. They may be a blessing coming here at this time do to the meeting of the leaders and them wanting to bring women into the fold. Having women in his group before it was acceptable would show his being way ahead of the game and one whose foresight was way ahead of the whole.

In short it may move me up in the leadership. And then there's Mafer, making her my woman. She is one fine woman, way above the others and seems to be healthier, too. Maybe that's why they made her their leader. But what woman wouldn't want to be the wife of the commander who soon may be the future leader?

Willow was lying in her sleeping bag with her hands behind her head and thinking about the man she had just met, the commander. So this was the man who gave the orders to have Bart killed? A nice-looking man really, at six foot, over two hundred pounds, beard as they all had, not bad. Too bad she had to kill him, and there was no doubt she would. She couldn't kill him in his camp with all his men around, but she had three whole days to make it happen. Anything could happen in that length of time; all she had to do was bide her time.

Chapter 8

THE NEXT MORNING the commander summoned Willow and made her a proposition. "How would you like to be part of my group, not a love slave but equals, as fighters?"

Willow looked at him and said, "Equals!"

"Yes, and no, it depends if you are fighting for the cause or not. I think you and your women would make an excellent addition to my group. I know you can all fight."

He went on to tell her about the meeting in the next few days of all the section leaders and what they were proposing.

"If you come with me, already in my group, that would go a long way into showing them that I'm already ahead of the game."

"And me, what does that do for me?"

"As my woman, you would be held in the highest regards."

"As your woman?"

The commander shook his head yes.

"Let me think about it. We've still got a couple of days. Plus it'll give me time to speak to the others."

"Take your time. You've got two days. In the meantime, I have to prepare my route to the meeting and who I'll be taking."

"Everyone's not going?"

"No, I won't need everyone. Maybe five men. If you and your women come, that'll be eleven, more than enough. The area where we're going is friendly. We should be OK."

Willow left the meeting with the commander and returned to her area and the other women, told them of the commander's proposition, and asked them what they thought. A couple of the women had mentioned they had fallen for two of the men in the camp and that before they departed, they should know whether or not they wanted to stay with them. Then they asked Willow what she was going to do, and she said that she had thoughts of going along with the commander; after all staying here in the mountains where it was cold as hell at night and simmering in the day just wasn't going to get it. Most of the women said that they'd go along with her.

I must be living right, Willow thought. *Going to that meeting will give me the perfect opportunity to accomplish my mission. I don't want to lay up with him, the person that had my man killed, but if I have to, I will. Two days, just two more days.*

Chapter 9

GENERAL HEADQUARTERS, Bravo division. Afghanistan.

General Housing and Colonel Morris were discussing the upcoming meeting with the leaders. The spotters for the drones would consist of three men. A helicopter would drop them off, and they would hike the rest of the way, which will be approximately ten miles. In so doing, they would have to avoid the unfriendliness. This drone hit was essential for the direction of the war and would take out some of the top of the clan. The good thing was there were no civilians in that area, and they would not have to worry about collateral damage. They shouldn't have to get any closer than three miles to the camp; once the spotters set it up, the drone would do the rest.

"Be advised," the general said. "An agent is believed to be in the area. If possible, give her all the assistance you can. From what they say, she may be anywhere in Afghanistan. Five foot eleven, black, speaks fluent Afghanistan, very capable in what she does. From what they say, if she's in the area, she'll probably find the spotters first. In case that happens, she'll know these code words: Alpha/tango/rainbow/Willow(ATRW)." The spotters were told the code.

"She won't be in that meeting, will she?"

The colonel said, "No, I don't think so. Women are not allowed in meetings like that. Never have been anyway."

"Sir, I was just thinking, if there is any chance that agent is going to be there, are we still going to bomb?"

"We are, Colonel. It's one life versus hundreds. Her superiors will understand."

"Who are the spotters you are sending?" the general asked.

"Master Sergeant Horn, Staff Sergeant Booker, and Corporal Dinkins. All are good men, capable men. All have had three or more tours over here. If the agent's there and they can, they'll bring her out, but then again, General, we may be jumping the gun. Afghanistan is a large country. What are the odds we run into her?"

"You're right, Colonel, but we'll still be on the lookout for her."

Two days later, the commander and his five men, and Willow and her four women—two had decided to stay in the camp with the men they had taken a liking to—set out. The commander told Willow it would take at least a day to reach the rendezvous point if everything went as planned. Willow was thinking and wondering where she could kill the commander before they reached the meeting place. There were still five men with him, and even if she were to eliminate them, there still were her people. She didn't know how they'd react to her killing him. There was a chance they'd go along with her, but she wasn't willing to take that chance.

Late that evening, they ran into ISIS, a group that had been feuding for years, and the commander didn't want a confrontation with them, not knowing how many men they had. Therefore, he said that they should take a long berth around them. It took them another half day to reach the camp.

Chapter 10

THE MEETING HAD been underway a good thirty minutes before the commander walked in. He gave his apologies, and they said that they understood. The elders consisted of nine men, the eldest being in his seventies. The group was sitting around a fire on pillows in the middle of the tent. Some were smoking pipes, and others were drinking coffee. There was one spot left, and that was for the commander.

Willow and the others were set up around a fire of their own, drinking coffee and eating. They had made it to the camp around ten that night. It had started getting colder, so Willow had a blanket around her with her AR-15 between her legs. The camp held fifty to sixty men and maybe ten or so women, not including Willow's crew.

Willow believed she had missed her chance to kill the commander; she had to wait a little longer. One of the men from the camp came over to one of Willow's women and started to talk to her. Willow couldn't hear what they were saying, but the woman got up and moved to another location. The other men saw what was happening and laughed at him. He didn't take that very well, so he followed her to where she was sitting, grabbed her hand, and pulled her up to him.

When she came up, it was with an eighteen-inch curved dagger, and she cut the man across the face, giving him a gash three inches long. He jumped back, releasing her and grabbing at his cheek; he saw the blood and grabbed for his weapon.

Willow and the other women saw what he was about to do, and they all pointed their weapons at him. He saw the women, stopped what he was about to do, turned around, and looked at his fellow Talibans, who were looking at the situation and not moving. Willow's women had their safeties on, but upon pointing it at him, they took them off. The man just stood there, bleeding, put a scarf over the cut, turned around, and returned to where he had been sitting.

The woman he had tried to accustom sat back down and cleaned her knife on her blanket. All the women put their weapons back beneath their blankets. When all was thought to be forgotten, everyone was back to drinking coffee and having their individual conversations.

Willow spotted him first, jumping up, grabbing his weapon, screaming, and heading for the woman, firing all the while. Willow pulled out her AR-15, took off the safety, and fired, putting six rounds into him. The other girls also fired at him, putting numerous holes into him but not before he had killed the woman he had sights on.

The leaders all came rushing out the tent, weapons in hand, wanting to know what happened, expecting the worst. It was explained to them what had happened, and it was within their rights to protect themselves.

Willow spoke for the group. Among other things she said was: "We are women who are willing to fight along with you, our men. But we are not willing to be disrespected. We are all women of martyrs, and we deserve more respect than that. Now we are wondering whether or not you deserve our respect."

The elder leader took all this in and told his men to take this trash into the desert and bury him. The leaders returned to the tent, and when there, he turned to the commander and asked, "Are the women with you?"

"Yes," he said. "I found them to be excellent fighters, and I wanted them with me. The leader was promised to Japel, my second-in-command, but he was killed, so she believes she's the wife of a martyr, even though they never married."

"We didn't get to that on our agenda, but if all the women handle themselves like your people, then I'm for recruiting as many as we can. You did great work, Commander, ahead of your time. There is a spot opening for an additional leader. You may be that one, Commander."

Later on that night, a group of Taliban bought in two Americans servicemen. They informed the leader that there had been three, but one was killed. The ones they captured were beat up some, and one was wounded.

The leaders said, "Commander, this is when your women earn their keep. Until the morning, they'll stand guard over the prisoners. They can try to find what they were doing in this area."

Willow and her group took the men into a tent that was set up nearby, tied them up, and saw to the wounded. There were only three—including Willow—left in her group after the one had gotten killed. Willow told two to get some sleep, and she would wake one up in two hours. She would take first shift.

Once she was alone with the men, she asked them what they were doing in the area and what their mission was. They said nothing.

"You will talk, you know. We have time."

"When did the Taliban use women fighting with them?" Sergeant Horn said.

In English Willow said, "Alpha-Tango-Rainbow-Willow."

Both men's eyes popped open wide, and they said, "What did you say?"

She repeated (ATR) Willow. Then they begin talking, telling why they were there and that before they were captured, they had been able to hide their equipment. They never expected to find her but were told to be on the lookout for her. They thought they'd be saving her, not the other way around.

"Well, don't count your chickens. We still need to get out of here. We've got a little over an hour."

One asked, "Is the meeting still going on?"

"The meeting will be on for hours. Let me cut you lose. We'll go out the back and into the mountains, and hopefully we can get back to your equipment and complete your mission."

"Have you completed yours yet?"

"No, maybe when you complete your mission, it'll help me complete mine."

Within two hours, they were back at the spot they were captured. No alert had been given. Willow felt it was due to her relief not waking up. The spotters found their equipment and set it up, and they called in the drone. The target was a direct hit, and the fireball could be seen for miles away. Willow felt bad for the women she left behind, but shit happens. They picked up the body of the third spotter and called in to be picked up.

Three hours later they were back at headquarters, and Willow was debriefed, and within two days on her way out of the country. A week later, she was in Washington, DC, and the office of agents Jenkins and Stone.

"Agent Willow, I was sorry to hear about Agent Bart. We brought his body back and buried him in Arlington National Cemetery. We know his death hit you hard, but you were informed to take no action."

"I don't recall you telling me that specifically. We must have lost contact before you did."

"OK, OK, let's leave it at that. All and all everything turned out OK, and you even saved a couple servicemen in the process. The commander is no more, and the camp was just about wiped out when we did our flyby. There were only a few people walking around. Great job!"

"You do get a vacation. Decided where you're going?"

"Maybe to Jamaica, get a little sun."

"Looks like you got enough sun in Afghanistan," Stone said. "You looking awful dark or dare I say, black."

"You know what they say, Agent Stone. The blacker the berry, the sweeter the juice."

Epilogue

JAMAICA has some of the most beautiful beaches in the world and some of the most beautiful women, Willow being one. The men weren't half-bad, either. Laying there in the shade under an umbrella and drinking a gin and tonic, she was wearing a bikini that was way too skimpy, a pair of Foster Grants shades, and her halter was untied with breasts totally visible. Her skin, ebony and gleaming, beautiful. After all this was Jamaica and anything goes. Men were walking by her, some three or four times. Willow paid them no mind because she was used to being stared at but kept watching the water and the sunset. The waiter dropped her drink twice. She forgave him, and he delivered her a double the next time around and used a larger tray.

They had given her two weeks, and she would make the most of them unless some kind of emergency came up, and it always did.

Where to this next time? Who will I meet? Who will I kill? And I will kill someone. I always have, and I always will until I'm stopped, and I don't see that happening. Call me naïve, but I believe I can't be killed. Maybe that's why I've lasted as long as I have. Besides the problem I have, I literally have a license to kill, a black 007, you might say. A perfect job for me. I love it. I miss Bart, and if I could have loved somebody, if I could have had feelings for anybody, it would have been Bart. In the meantime, I must satisfy the body, and the dead can't do that.

Reunion

Willow had her eyes closed when she felt someone kiss her on the cheek, and just before she was about to give the person a hi-ya, Jesse said, "Janice, I would have recognized those breasts anywhere. What the hell you doing here in Jamaica?"

"Jesse Bo-T, well, I'll be damned. Jesse, how long has it been? A couple of years at least."

"Janice, you still with the company?"

"Yeah, I'm still with the company, Jesse. What are you doing now, and have you seen Dorothy lately?"

Willow sat up and turned around for Jesse to tie her halter.

"The last time I saw her, she was in Hawaii and had married this high roller about twice her age."

"Dorothy was near forty-three or forty-four herself. This guy must have been near dead."

"Yeah," Jesse said, "but knowing her, I'll bet she had a plan."

Janice put her arms around Jesse and said, "Jesse, it's sure good to see you again."

The guys that were walking by at the time Willow was hugging Jesse said, "Lucky mother jump."

Jesse was a player, and occasionally he ran drugs. He liked the ladies, and the ladies liked him. Five foot eight, one hundred seventy pounds, brown skin, black eyes, and curly black hair. Thin black mustache and a small cut on the corner of his mouth. A cute little guy, Willow had always thought. There was only one woman that she knew he was crazy about, really crazy about, Samantha!

"Are you working, Janice, or on vacation or what?"

"No, I'm on vacation, Jesse. Just out here chilling, as you can see. How about us getting together later for dinner, catching up on old times?"

"You got it, Janice. I got a little mama over here I was on my way to."

"You still running the ladies, Jesse? You never slowed down?"

"You know me, Janice. Where you staying?"

Jesse, Dorothy, and Willow had worked together some years back. She had gotten really close to them, but they never wanted to stay with the company like her. The company had gotten Dorothy out of prison after she served five years for killing her boyfriend's girlfriend. They were about to put Jesse in prison for going AWOL from the military and skipping out with the drugs and money of those he was working for. They—the Feds—made all of them an offer that they couldn't refuse.

They succeeded in closing out that case in record time and three more after that. Jesse was never too much into the job, but he did it, and they all got pardons after the jobs were done, except Willow. They informed her in no uncertain terms that they would never let her go; she wondered why.

It would be nice getting together with Jesse again. Janice knew he would have some stories to tell.

Meanwhile in Hawaii, Dorothy's husband had died, and she was at the funeral. Many people were there, and she was glad when it was over. She knew few of the people there anyway. They had been married less than two years but long enough for Dorothy to convince him to change his will and leave everything to her, a little over $200 million. Now her retirement was assured.

They had, or he had, homes all over the place—Alaska, England, and there in Hawaii and one in Jamaica. They had just been in England six months ago and hunting in Alaska this past February. That was where he got pneumonia. So to get away from all those headaches, she thought she'd go to Jamaica this time. All she had to do was contact her pilot, call the staff there, let them know she would be going, and go. Her lawyers would have to go there to finalize everything. They had mentioned something about double indemnity insurance; in that case, she would think about replacing her aircraft.

It's settled then, she thought. *Jamaica it is.*

A week later in Agent Jenkins office, Agent Stone was saying, "I don't know, sir, what we're going to do. Everyone seems to be tied up with Afghanistan and Iran and other commitments. I've never seen it this bad since 9/11. For this next assignment, we're going to need at least three agents."

"I know we promised Janice a long vacation, but it looks like we're not going to be able to honor that promise," Jenkins said. "Even if we recruit her for this one, she'll need help. Any ideas?"

"I've been thinking about it, sir; you remember that first assignment we sent her on? Well, there were two other people with her, a Dorothy Malone and Jesse Bo-T. They did a hell of a job on that one and just about closed the operation down completely. Besides that, there were three other assignments that they did well on also."

"We need that team back together again; do you think we can locate them?"

"Well, sir, we know where Janice is, and I'm sure she can find the others. She did it before. I'll get right on it, sir."

Al Ham Bra Club, Jamaica. Jesse and Janice were sitting at a table in the middle of the room. Janice was wearing a low-cut white evening gown with white pearls and earrings. Her hair was up in a bun with a diamond stickpin on top. The rings on her fingers were mostly diamonds, but there was one surrounded with pearls and a ruby in the middle. The last was a figure of Midas's head with rubies as eyes. There was also a duplicate of that figure on her backside that only certain people ever saw. Jesse had a tuxedo on and the bling.

The club was packed due to the show they had; Natalie Cole, Al Jarreau, and George Benson were headlining. Plus, a band of national acclaim. The show went on without a hitch for two hours, and they enjoyed themselves immensely. They laughed and cried and patted their feet to the music. When the show was over, they were spent and happy. The lights came on, and they ordered another drink.

Jesse nudged Janice and said, "Look there."

Across the room, wearing a black silk dress, open at the sleeves, and three-inch-high heels. Diamond rings on her fingers; necklace and earrings and watch to match. Five foot eleven—over six foot with the heels—light skin, and long legs. It was Dorothy Malone coming their way and smiling.

At forty-four Dorothy was a beautiful woman. She was dressed like she had a million bucks, and her posture was that of someone who had been in the military, which she had. Standing tall proud and in control of her destiny.

"Janice, Jesse," she said, after hugging and kissing them both. "This is really a surprise. Never thought I'd see you two again."

After trading niceties, they went quiet and just looked at one another, remembering the cases they had been on and how it all began.

"Are you still with the agency?" Dorothy asked Willow.

"You know I'm not going anyplace," Janice answered, "even if I wanted to."

"What about you, Jesse?"

"Oh, hell no. I need my freedom. The last time I was involved, well, you remember."

"Did you ever get together with Samantha?"

"Yes, and no. You know how she looked when we were on that first case and we rescued her? The most beautiful girl I had ever seen. Then on that next case when I was supposed to meet her again…hell, that was the only reason I agreed to help out. After we closed the case, I waited for her down in the barrio just like Janice said. She was supposed to show up at around eleven or twelve p.m. within three nights. After all kinds of people coming up to my car, wine heads, prostitutes, panhandlers, and whatever. Glad I had my piece on me. Almost shot me a sucker.

"Anyway on the last night, about twelve p.m., I was about to call it and chalk it up as a no-show when this bag lady comes up to me and asked me for money. Now, this same woman had come up to me before. In fact the last three nights about the same time. She was pushing a grocery cart, wearing a long, oversize coat, shoes that one would wear in the circus. Big, floppy hat with hair underneath and dreadlocks to her shoulders. By this time, I'm mad as hell about Samantha not showing up and this woman bugging me. So I gave her five bucks just to get her the hell out of my face, and then she started complaining about the amount I gave her. She thought it should have been more.

"At this time, I was about ready to really explode and told her she better get the hell out of my face when she says, 'Jesse, don't you recognize me? Have I changed that much?'

"I stopped right there and said, 'Recognize who?' I'm really looking at this bitch now. I raised up in my seat, stuck my head out the window, and said, 'Samantha?'"

"She was undercover?" Janice asked.

"Yes, she was undercover. Fooled the hell out of me, but once we got to my hotel room and she took a bath and removed all that bullshit…Samantha in the flesh. It was worth it, all of it."

Then it was Dorothy's turn. She told of traveling around the Caribbean, meeting different men, and finally meeting one elderly man who took a liking to her and decided he wanted to marry her. Found out he was worth some $200 million, and he didn't push for a nuptial agreement, against his lawyer's advice, because he had no family and was in his eighties. He died, and now she had it all, but it was still not like when they were all together. It seemed like that was when she felt more alive. Maybe it was the adrenaline. She didn't know, but she hadn't felt like that since.

Then it was Janice's turn. She told of the assignments since she had been with them, the assignments to the Swiss Alps, with stops in Korea and Texas. The meeting with the pimp "Smooth" in Alaska and him introducing her to a detective named Ruben Kane.

"All this for the agency?" Jesse asked.

"Yes, all that for the agency," Janice said.

"Hey, I tell you what: the show's over, so let's get out of here. I want you two to see my home."

"You have a home here in Jamaica?" Jesse asked.

"Sure do, and you won't believe it."

"Dorothy, with the kind of money you have, I know you wouldn't mind letting a brother borrow a few bucks."

"Name it, Jesse, and it's yours."

Outside the club, Dorothy's limo, driven by a fine-looking Jamaican female of twenty-two, picked them up. As the old friends sat themselves in the back, Dorothy offered them a drink from a small bar.

Willow's cell rang. Looking at the caller ID, she saw that it was Agent Stone.

"Janice, I'm sorry to bother you on your vacation, but we have a situation."

"How nice," Willow said.

"Do you think you could locate Dorothy and Jesse? You'll need them for this next assignment if they'll agree."

Willow looked at both Dorothy and Jesse, and they looked back at her and said, "What?"

Other books by this author:

Enlisted at 14…A Memoir
Enlisted at 14 and the Journey Continues
Enlisted at 14…Looking Back

Willow…A Novel
Willow…One for the Team
Willow…And the Medusa
Little Miss Willow…A Short Story
Assassin

Meet Ruben Kane
R.K. {Ruben Kane}
Ruben's Bag
Ruben's Bad Side
Smooth…A Ruben Kane Novel
Mo Kane
Dear Client
And Then Some
Ducks in a Row

Just a Dream

Dream Catcher

www.ingramcontent.com/pod-product-compliance
Lightning Source LLC
Chambersburg PA
CBHW070810120626
46557CB00002B/795